Charles Kirkpatrick Sharpe, Edmund Marsdon Goldsmid

Ballads of Books

Or, Popular and Romantic Ballads and Songs Current in Annandale and...

Charles Kirkpatrick Sharpe, Edmund Marsdon Goldsmid

Ballads of Books
Or, Popular and Romantic Ballads and Songs Current in Annandale and...

ISBN/EAN: 9783744773287

Printed in Europe, USA, Canada, Australia, Japan

Cover: Foto ©Andreas Hilbeck / pixelio.de

More available books at **www.hansebooks.com**

A

BALLAD BOOK.

She thrusts her right hand into the very bottom of his pannier.—"I have nothing, good Lady, but empty bottles!" says the ass.—SLAWKENBERGIUS.

A

Bibliotheca Curiosa.

A

BALLAD BOOK;

OR,

POPULAR AND ROMANTIC BALLADS AND
SONGS CURRENT IN ANNANDALE AND
OTHER PARTS OF SCOTLAND.

COLLECTED BY

CHARLES KIRKPATRICK SHARPE.

Reprinted from the Rare Original Edition of 1824,

and Edited by

EDMUND GOLDSMID, F.R.H.S.

PART I.

PRIVATELY PRINTED, EDINBURGH.

1883.

This Edition is limited to seventy-five Large Paper copies, and two hundred and seventy-five Small Paper copies, issued only to Subscribers.

UNWIN BROTHERS, PRINTERS, LONDON AND CHILWORTH.

INTRODUCTION.

THE collection of Ballads here reprinted is well known by name to all lovers of this class of Ancient Poetry, but the book itself can have been seen by few. Privately printed in 1824 for distribution among the Editor's friends, only thirty copies issued from the press, and, of these, half at least have found a permanent resting-place on the shelves of our large public or semi-public Libraries.*

The Editor was one of a band of quaint Antiquarian *Littérateurs*, which included Maidment,† Kinloch,‡ Buchan,§ &c., who devoted much time and labour to rescuing these unwritten traditions of the land, at the very period when they were sinking into oblivion. Gathered, as he tells us, from the mouths of nurses, wet and dry, dairy-

---

* A copy fetched £6 17s. 6d. at Mr. J. Maidment's sale.

† Editor of "A New Book of Old Ballads," "A North Countrie Garland," &c., &c.

‡ Editor of "The Ballad Book."

§ Editor of "Ancient Ballads and Songs of the North of Scotland."

maids, and tenants' daughters, it is not surprising if in form they are often rough and uncouth, and in ideas not always over-delicate. But, notwithstanding all their faults, nay, for that very reason, they will not fail to interest all who yet value

> The songs, to savage virtue dear,
> That won of yore the public ear,
> Ere polity, sedate and sage,
> Had quench'd the fires of Feudal rage.

"Give me the writing of the Ballads, and you may make the Laws," cried Fletcher of. Saltoun, and he was right. Alfred for generations probably owed as much of his fame to the Ballads he wrote* as to the laws he "adapted," to use our modern dramatic expression, from Ethelbert, Ina, or Offa. The minstrel has been in turn protected by Edward of York and treated as a rogue and a vagabond by his illustrious great grand-daughter ;† Richard Cœur-de-Lion is perhaps better known as a Troubadour than as the Conqueror of Cyprus ; generation after generation of our peasantry have cheered the long winter evenings, and listened with awe to the tale of Rothiemay, or the fate of "Fause Sir John"; Governments have quaked at the sound of "Lilliburlero," or "Ça ira."

---

* William of Malmesbury's Chronicles.

† Viner's "General Abridgment of the Laws of England."

In " A Ballad Book," at least five ballads were printed for the first time, viz.—

> Lady Dysmal.
> Glasgow Peggie.
> Fair Margaret of Craignargat.
> O Errol it's a bonny place.
> Ritchie Storie.

I have printed Mr. Sharpe's book word for word, only altering the position of his notes from the beginning to the end of each Ballad;* giving a name to such Ballads as had had none assigned them ; adding a Table of Contents ; and, lastly, subjoining such notes as seemed to me *really* necessary. I have always held that too many notes impede rather than help the reader, and I have acted in accordance with my opinion.

EDMUND GOLDSMID.

EDINBURGH, *Oct. 12th*, 1883.

---

* The *original* nc   are distinguished throughout by the initials *C.K.S.*

ORIGINAL PREFACE.

As this book, of which only thirty copies are printed, shall cost thee nothing, save a little time thrown away on its perusal, which most Antiquaries can very well spare, I will make no apology to thee for the compiling of it. The truth is, I was anxious after this fashion, to preserve a few songs that afforded me much delight in my early youth, and are not to be found at all, or complete, or in the same shape in other Collections. These have been mostly gathered from the mouths of nurses, wet and dry, singing to their babes and sucklings, dairy-maids pursuing their vocation in the cow-house, and tenants' daughters, while giving the Lady (as every Laird's wife was once called) a spinning day, whilom an anniversary tribute in Annandale. Several, too, were picked up from tailors, who were wont to reside in my father's castle, while misshaping clothes for the children and servants. Though I am sensible that none of these Ballads are of much merit, I regret that my memory doth not now serve me as to many more, the outlines of which alone I remember. Some, indeed, I have suppressed on account of their grossness; confessing, at the same time, that several here printed are not over delicate; but little will be found to corrupt the imagination, and nothing to inflame the passions. Sufficit! I have inserted a few from MS. Collections in my possession, and perhaps shall be tempted by and by to add a second volume from the same sources. In the mean time, gentle reader,

HAIL! AND FAREWELL!

INDEX TO PART I.

A BALLAD BOOK.

I.

FAIR JANET.*

" YE maun gang to your father, Janet,
 Ye maun gang to him soon ;
Ye maun gang to your father, Janet,
 In case that his days are dune ! "

Janet's awa' to her father,
 As fast as she could hie ;
" O, what's your will wi' me, father?
 O, what's your will wi' me ? "

" My will wi' you, fair Janet," he said,
 " It is both bed and board ;
Some say that ye lo'e sweet Willie,
 But ye maun wed a French lord."

---

* This ballad, the subject of which appears to have been
very popular, is printed as it was sung by an old woman in
Perthshire. The air is extremely beautiful.—C. K. S. It
is usually printed under the title of " Willie and Annet,"
and was also published by Mr. Finlay in an improved (?)
version, under the title of " Sweet Willie."

"A French lord maun I wed, father?
  A French lord maun I wed?
Then by my sooth," quo fair Janet,
  "He's neer enter my bed."

Janet's awa' to her chamber,
  As fast as she could go ;
Wha's the first ane that tapped there,
  But sweet Willie, her jo?

"O we maun part this love, Willie,
  That has been lang between ;
There's a French lord coming o'er the sea,
  To wed me wi' a ring ;
There's a French lord coming o'er the sea,
  To wed and tak' me hame."

"If we maun part this love, Janet,
  It causeth mickle woe ;
If we maun part this love, Janet,
  It makes me into mourning go."

"But ye maun gang to your three sisters,
  Meg, Marion, and Jean ;
Tell them to come to fair Janet,
  In case that her days are dune."

Willie's awa' to his three sisters,
  Meg, Marion and Jean ;
"O, haste and gang to fair Janet,
  I fear that her days are dune."

Some drew to them their silken hose,
　　Some drew to them their shoon,
Some drew to them their silk manteils,
　　Their coverings to put on ;
And they're awa' to fair Janet,
　　By the hie light o' the moon.

*　　*　　*　　*　　*

" O, I have born this babe, Willie,
　　Wi' mickle toil and pain ;
Take hame, take hame your babe, Willie,
　　For nurse I dare be nane."

He's tane his young son in his arms,
　　And kiss't him cheek and chin—
And he's awa' to his mother's bower,
　　By the hie light o' the moon.

"O, open, open, mother," he says,
　　"O, open, and let me in ;
The rain rains on my yellow hair,
　　And the dewdrops o'er my chin—
And I hae my young son in my arms,
　　I fear that his days are dune."

With her fingers lang and sma',
　　She lifted up the pin ;
And with her arms lang and sma',
　　Received the baby in.

" Gae back, gae back, now sweet Willie,
    And comfort your fair lady ;
For where ye had but ae nourice,
    Your young son shall hae three."

Willie he was scarce awa'
    And the lady put to bed,
When in and came her father dear,
    "Make haste and busk the bride."

"There's a sair pain in my head, father,
    There's a sair pain in my side,
And ill, O ill, am I, father,
    This day for to be a bride."

"O, ye maun busk this bonny bride,
    And put a gay mantle on ;
For she shall wed this auld French lord,
    Gin she should die the morn."

Some pat on the gay green robes,
    And some pat on the brown,
But Janet put on the scarlet robes
    To shine foremost throw the town.

And some they mounted the black steed,
    And some mounted the brown,
But Janet mounted the milk-white steed
    To ride foremost throw the town.

" O, wha will guide your horse, Janet ?
  O, wha will guide him best ? "
" O, wha but Willie, my true love,
  He kens I lo'e him best ! "

And whan they came to Marie's kirk,
  To tye the haly ban,
Fair Janet's cheek looked pale and wan,
  And her colour gaed an cam.

When dinner it was past and done,
  And dancing to begin ;
" O, we'll go take the bride's maidens,
  And we'll go fill the ring."

O, ben than cam' the auld French lord,
  Saying, " Bride, will ye dance wi' me ? "
" Awa', awa', ye auld French lord,
  Your face I downa see."

O, ben than cam' now sweet Willie,
  He cam' with ane advance ;
" O, I'll go tak' the bride's maidens,
  And we'll go tak' a dance."

" I've seen ither days wi' you, Willie,
  And so has mony mae ;
Ye would hae dance wi' me mysel',
  Let a' my maidens gae."

B

O, ben than cam' now sweet Willie,
    Saying, " Bride, will ye dance wi' me ? "
" Aye, by my sooth, and that I will,
    Gin my back should break in three."

She had nae turned her throw the dance,
    Throw the dance but thrice,
Whan she fell doun at Willie's feet,
    And up did never rise !

Willie's ta'en the key of his coffer,
    And gi'en it to his man,
" Gae hame, and tell my mother dear,
    My horse he has me slain ;
Bid her be kind to my young son,
    For father he has nane."

The tane was buried in Marie's kirk
    And the tither in Marie's quier ;
Out of the tane there grew a birk,
    And the tither a bonny brier.

II.

THE LASSES O' THE CANNOGATE.*

The lasses o' the Cannogate, †
O' they are wondrous nice,
They winna gie a single kiss
But for a double price.

Gar hang them, gar hang them,
Heich upon a tree,
For we'll get better up the gate
For a bawbee.

III.

THE VAIN GUDEWIFE.

I'LL gar our gudeman trow
That I'll sell the ladle,
If he winna buy to me
A new side saddle
To ride to the kirk, and frae the kirk,
And round about the toun,—
Stand about, ye fisher jads,
And gie my goun room !

---

* The two following songs were remembered thirty years ago by an old gentlewoman. The first seems to be a satire on the Court ladies of Edinburgh.—C. K. S.

† A street in the old town of Edinburgh, a continuation of the High Street. It was once the fashionable quarter of the town.

I'll gar our gudeman trow
  That I'll tak' the fling strings,
If he winna buy to me
  Twelve bonnie goud rings,—
Ane for ilka finger,
  And twa for ilka thoom,—
Stand about, ye fisher jads,
  And gie my goun room !

I'll gar our gudeman trow
  That I'll tak' the glengore,
If he winna fee to me
  Three valets or four,
To beir my tail up frae the dirt,
  And ush me throw the toun,—
Stand about, ye fisher jads,
  And gie my goun room ! *

IV.

LADY DYSMAL.

THERE was a king, and a glorious king,
  And a king of mickle fame ;
And he had daughters only one,
  Lady Dysmal was her name.

---

* As illustrations of the above song, *vide* Sir Richard
Maitland's Poems, beginning :—
  "Some wyfis of the Borroustoun
    So wander vane are, and wantoun."
And also Sir David Lindsay's supplication against Syde
Taillis and Mussalit Faces.—C. K. S.

He had a boy, and a kitchen boy,
   A boy of mickle scorn ;
And she lov'd him lang, and she lov'd him
     aye,
   Till the grass o'ergrew the corn.

When twenty weeks were gone and past,
   O, she began to greet ;
Her petticoats grew short before,
   And her stays they wadna meet.

It fell upon a winter's night,
   The king could get nae rest ;
He cam unto his daughter dear,
   Just like a wand'ring ghaist.

He cam into her bed-chamber,
   And drew the curtains round,—
"What aileth thee, my daughter dear ?
   I fear you've gotten wrong."

" O, if I have, despise me not,
   For he is all my joy ;
I will forsake baith dukes and earls,
   And marry your kitchen boy.''

" Go call to me my merry men all,
   By thirty and by three ;
Go call to me my kitchen boy,
   We'll murder him secretlie."

There was nae din that could be heard,
   And ne'er a word was said,
Till they got him baith fast and sure,
   Between twa feather beds.

" Go, cut the heart out of his breast,
   And put it in a cup of gold ;
And present it to his Dysmal dear,
   For she is baith stout and bold."

They've cut the heart out of his breast,
   And put it in a cup of gold ;
And presented it to his Dysmal dear,
   Who was baith stout and bold.

" O, come to me, my hinney, my heart,
   O, come to me, my joy ;
O, come to me, my hinney, my heart,
   My father's kitchen boy."

She's ta'en the cup out of their hands,
   And set it at her bed head ;
She wash'd it wi' the tears that fell from her
    eyes,
   And next morning she was dead.

" O, where were ye, my merry men all,
   Whom I paid meat and wage,
Ye didna hold my cruel hand,
   Whan I was in my rage ?"

" For gone is a' my heart's delight,
    And gone is a' my joy ;
For my dear Dysmal she is dead,
    And so is my kitchen boy."*

V.

THE BRIDEGROOM.

THERE lived a man into the west,
    And O ! but he was cruel ;
Upon his waddin' nicht at e'en,
    He sat up and grat for gruel.

They brought to him a good sheep's head,
    A napkin, and a towel,—
" Gae tak' your whim-whams a' frae me,
    And bring me fast my gruel."

---

* This stupid ballad, printed as it was sung in Annandale, is founded on the well-known story of the Prince of Salerno's daughter; but with what uncouth change ! Dysmal for Ghismonda, and Guiscardo transformed into a greasy kitchen boy :
      " An ounce of civet, good apothecary,
        To sweeten my imagination."
The reader will immediately remember Hogarth's picture and Churchill's exclamation :—
    " Poor Sigismunda, what a fate was thine !"—C. K. S.
Compare also the " Story of a Lover's Heart " in Disraeli's " Curiosities of Literature."

The BRIDE *speaks.*

" There is nae meal into the hous,
    What shall I do, my jewel ?"
" Gae to the pock and shake a lock,
    For I canna want my gruel."

" There is nae milk into the hous,
    What shall I do, my jewel ?"
" Gae to the midden and milk the soo,
    For I wunna want my gruel."*

VI.

MARIE HAMILTON.

WORD'S gane to the kitchen
    And word's gane to the ha',
That Marie Hamilton gangs wi' bairn
    To the hichest Stewart of a'.

He's courted her in the kitchen,
    He's courted her in the ha',
He's courted her in the laigh cellar,
    And that was warst of a' !

---

* This song, from some original words of the air to which
Auld Robin Gray was latterly adapted, appears to have
been composed on a similar melancholy event.
" The bridegroom grat when the sun gaed down   (*Repeat*)
And ' Och,' quo' he, ' It's come o'er soon,'" &c.—C. K. S.

She's tyed it in her apron,
   And she's thrown it in the sea,
Says "Sink ye, swim ye, bonny wee babe,
   You'l ne'er get mair o' me."

Down then cam' the auld Queen,
   Goud tassels tying her hair,
"O, Marie, where's the bonny wee babe,
   That I heard greet sae sair?"

"There was never a babe intill my room,
   As little designs to be;
It was but a touch o' my sair side,
   Come o'er my fair bodie."

"O, Marie, put on your robes o' black,
   Or else your robes o' brown,
For ye maun gang wi' me the night,
   To see fair Edinbro' town."

"I winna put on my robes o' black,
   Nor yet my robes o' brown,
But I'll put on my robes o' white,
   To shine through Edinbro' town."

When she gaed up the Cannogate,
   She laugh'd loud laughters three;
But whan she cam down the Cannogate,
   The tear blinded her e'e.

When she gaed up the Parliament stair,
  The heel cam aff her shee,
And lang or she cam down again,
  She was condemn'd to dee.

When she cam down the Cannogate,
  The Cannogate sae free,
Mony a ladie look'd o'er her window,
  Weeping for this ladie.

" Ye need nae weep for me," she says,
  " Ye need nae weep for me,
For had I not slain mine own sweet babe,
  This death I wadna dee.

" Bring me a bottle of wine," she says,
  " The best that e'er ye hae,
That I may drink to my weil wishers,
  And they may drink to me.

" Here's a health to the jolly sailors,
  That sail upon the main,
Let them never let on to my father and
    mother,
  But what I'm coming hame.

" Here's a health to the jolly sailors
  That sail upon the sea ;
Let them never let on to my father and
    mother,
  That I am here to dee.

"Oh, litttle did my mother think,
  The day she cradled me,
What lands I was to travel through,
  What death I was to dee.

"Oh, little did my father think,
  The day he held up me,
What lands I was to travel through,
  What death I was to dee.

"Last night I wash'd the Queen's feet,
  And gently laid her down ;
And a' the thanks I've gotten the nicht,
  To be hang'd in Edinbro' town.

"Last nicht there was four Maries,
  The nicht there'l be but three ;
There was Marie Seton, and Marie Beton,
  And Marie Carmichael, and me."*

---

* In the Border Minstrelsy (vol. iii. page 87) is a much
more refined edition of this ballad, which is supposed to
relate the misadventure of one of Queen Marie's ladies. It
is singular that during the reign of the Czar Peter, one of
his Empress's attendants, a Miss Hamilton (spelt Hamble-
ton by Sir Walter Scott), was executed for the murder of a
natural child,—not her first crime in that way, as was
suspected ; and the Czar, whose admiration of her beauty
did not preserve her life, stood upon the scaffold till her
head was struck off, which he lifted by the ear, and kissed
on the lips. I cannot help thinking that the two stories
have been confused in the ballad, for if Marie Hamilton was
executed in Scotland, it is not likely that her relations

VII.

LADY DUNDONALD.

WEEL it becomes the Lady Dundonald,
  To sit liltin' at her rock,
And weel it becomes the Laird of Dundonald,
  To wear his hodden gray frock !
    Chorus.—Lilty eery, lardy lardy
      Lilty eery, lardy lam.

(*Enter* MARG'ET.)

" My Lady, there is a lass at the door wants to be
    feed."
  " What fee does she want ? "   " Five punds."
" Five punds is o'er mony punds, to be
  Drawing out the tail o' a rock."
    Chorus.—Lilty, eery, &c.

" Tell her I will gee her four punds,
  And spin a' the backs mysel."
    Chorus.—Lilty, eery, &c.

---

resided beyond seas, and we have no proof that Hamilton
was really the name of the woman who made a slip with
Darnley.—C. K. S.   A third version is given by Motherwell,
as the one current in the west of Scotland (page 401) ; but
the most complete is that reprinted by the Aungervyle
Society (series 1, 1881).   In Knox's " History of the Reformation " (page 373-4), it is stated that the murderess was
a Frenchwoman in the Queen's suite, and the father of the
child the Queen's apothecary.   " This was the beginning
of the regiment of Mary, Queen of Scots, and these were
the fruits which she brought forth of France," exclaims the
bigoted Scotsman, with admirable love of justice !

(*Enter* MARG'ET.)

" My Lady, what will I tell you noo,
  Isna our kitchen lass wi' bairn !
What may that be till ?
  The Laird, I needna speir."
    Chorus.—Lilty eery, &c.

" He has fifteen at the fireside else,
And that will mak sixteen,
And sae it will een ;
It was me that made him a Laird ;
And deel speed sic Lairds !"
    Chorus.—Lilty eery, &c.

" Hear, Marg'et."   " What does my Lady want
          noo ? "
" Bring ben the brandy bottle, your waas,
And tak' a dram yoursel',
And gar we tak' twa."
    Chorus.—Lilty eery, &c.

" I think we may as weel
Tak' our ain geer oursels,
For it is gaein' whether or no."
    Chorus.—Lilty eery, &c.

(*Enter* JOHN.)

" My Lady, there is company come."
" Fashious fock, John ; I want nae company,
I am spinning at my rock."
    Chorus.—Lilty ecry, &c.

"M y Lady, the servants is going to their beds,
They want the doup of a candle."
" Tell them to put doups and doups thegither,
And that will gie them licht."*
  Chorus.—Lilty eery, &c.

VIII.

JENNY.

JENNY, scho's ta'en a deep surprise,
 And scho's spew'd a' her crowdie,
Her minnie scho ran to seek her a dram,
 But scho stude mair need o' the howdie.

" O, Sandie, dinna ye mind," quo' scho,
" Whan ye gart me drink the brandy,
Whan ye yerkit me ow'r amang the braume,
And plaid me Houghmagandy ! "

----

* This strange folly was generally sung by a man, with a woman's cap on his head, a distaff, and a spindle. The dialogue, of which the subjoined is only a fragment, was chanted in recitative. Can this song possibly allude to Elizabeth, daughter and heiress of William Cochrane of Cochrane, who married Alexander, a younger son of John Blair of Blair? Her father made a settlement of his estate in her favour 1593. At Gosford, a seat of the Earl of Wemyss, is a full-length portrait of a hideous old woman, with her spinning implements, and a starved cat, said to be the Lady Dundonald of the ballad, but to me it appears to be the figure of a Flemish peasant.—C. K. S.

IX.

DESERTED.

AND sae ye've treated me,
And sae ye've treated me ;
I'll never lo'e anither man,
Sae weil as I've lo'ed thee.
And sae ye've treated me,
And sae ye've treated me ;
The deil pit on your windin' sheet
Three hours before you dee !

X.

THE TWA SISTERS.

THERE liv'd twa sisters in a bower,
  Hey Edinbruch, how Edinbruch,
There liv'd twa sisters in a bower,
    Stirling for aye ;
The youngest o' them, O, she was a flower !
  Bonny Sanct Johnstoune that stands upon Tay.

There cam a squire frae the west,
  Hey Edinbruch, how Edinbruch,
There cam a squire frae the west,
    Stirling for aye ;
He lo'ed them baith, but the youngest best,
  Bonny Sanct Johnstoune that stands upon Tay.

He gied the eldest a gay gold ring,
   Hey Edinbruch, how Edinbruch,
He gied the eldest a gay gold ring,
     Stirling for aye ;
But he lo'ed the youngest aboon a' thing,
  Bonny Sanct Johnstoune that stands upon Tay.

"Oh, sister, sister, will ye go to the sea?
   Hey Edinbruch, how Edinbruch,
Oh, sister, sister, will ye go to the sea?
     Stirling for aye ;
Our father's ships sail bonnilie,
   Bonny Sanct Johnstoune that stands upon Tay."

The youngest sat down upon a stane,
   Hey Edinbruch, how Edinbruch,
The youngest sat down upon a stane,
     Stirling for aye ;
The eldest shot the youngest in,
   Bonny Sanct Johnstoune that stands upon Tay.

"Oh, sister, sister, lend me your hand,
   Hey Edinbruch, how Edinbruch,
Oh, sister, sister, lend me your hand,
     Stirling for aye ;
And you shall hae my gouden fan,
   Bonny Sanct Johnstoune that stands upon Tay.

"Oh, sister, sister, save my life,
   Hey Edinbruch, how Edinbruch,

Oh, sister, sister, save my life,
    Stirling for aye ;
And ye shall be the squire's wife,
    Bonny Sanct Johnstoune that stands upon Tay."

First she sank, and then she swam,
    Hey Edinbruch, how Edinbruch,
First she sank, and then she swam,
    Stirling for aye ;
Until she cam to Tweed mill dam,
    Bonny Sanct Johnstoune that stands upon Tay.

The millar's daughter was baking bread,
    Hey Edinbruch, how Edinbruch,
The millar's daughter was baking bread,
    Stirling for aye.
She went for water, as she had need,
    Bonny Sanct Johnstoune that stands upon Tay.

"Oh, father, father, in our mill dam,
    Hey Edinbruch, how Edinbruch,
Oh, father, father, in our mill dam,
    Stirling for aye ;
There's either a lady, or a milk-white swan,
    Bonny Sanct Johnstoune that stands upon Tay."

They could nae see her fingers small,
    Hey Edinbruch, how Edinbruch,
They could nae see her fingers small,
    Stirling for aye ;

Wi' diamond rings they were cover'd all,
　　Bonny Sanct Johnstoune that stands upon Tay·

They could nae see her yellow hair,
　　Hey Edinbruch, how Edinbruch,
They could nae see her yellow hair,
　　　　Stirling for aye ;
Sae mony knotts and platts war there,
　　Bonny Sanct Johnstoune that stands upon Tay.

They could nae see her lily feet,
　　Hey Edinbruch, how Edinbruch,
They could nae see her lilly feet,
　　　　Stirling for aye ;
Her gowden fringes war sae deep,
　　Bonny Sanct Johnstoune that stands upon Tay.

Bye there cam a fiddler fair,
　　Hey Edinbruch, how Edinbruch,
Bye there cam a fiddler fair,
　　　　Stirling for aye ;
And he's ta'en three taits o' her yellow hair,
　　Bonny Sanct Johnstoune that stands upon Tay.*

　　*　　＊　　＊　　＊　　＊

----

* Various sets of this song have been printed. It was popular both in England and Scotland. The air is beautiful.—C.K.S.

It is usually called " Binnorie," from the ordinary chorus. A version is given in the Border Minstrelsy, which is far more complete. A parody of it is to be found in D'Urfey's, " Pills to purge Melancholy."

XI.

THE FIDDLER'S BENISON.

My blessing gae wi' ye, Jock Rob, Jock Rob,
My blessing gae wi' you, Jock Rob ;
For whan ye come here, ye mak' us good cheer,
And gar our blythe bottoms play bob !

XII.

THE SOUTAR AND THE SOO.

The soutar gied the soo a kiss—
" Grumph," quo' scho, " it's for my briss."
" And whare gat ye sae sweet a mou ? "
Quo' the soutar to the soo.
" Grumph," quo' scho, " and whare gat ye
A tongue sae sleekie and sae slee ? "*

XIII.

GLENLOGIE.

Four and twenty nobles sits in the king's ha',
Bonnie Glenlogie is the flower among them a'.

In came Lady Jean skipping on the floor,
And she has chosen Glenlogie 'mong a' that was
    there.

---

* It is very strange, as well as amusing, to observe how much our ancient poets detested soutars. Examples are too numerous to be quoted.—C. K. S.

She turned to his footman, and thus she did say :
" Oh, what is his name, and where does he stay ?"

" IIis name is Glenlogie, when he is from home,
IIe is of the gay Gordons, his name it is John."

" Glenlogie, Glenlogie, an' you will prove kind,
My love is laid on you, I am telling my mind."

He turned about lightly, as the Gordons does a',
" I thank you, Lady Jean, my love is promised
  awa'."

She called on her maidens her bed for to make,
Her rings and her jewels all from her to take.

In came Jeanie's father, a wae man was he,
Says, " I'll wed you to Drumfendrich, he has mair
  gold than he."

IIer father's own chaplain, being a man of great
  skill,
He wrote him a letter, and indited it well ;

The first lines he looked at, a light laugh laughed
  he,
But ere he read through it, the tears blinded his
  e'e.

Oh, pale and wan looked she when Glenlogie cam'
in,

But even rosy grew she when Glenlogie sat down.

" Turn round, Jeanie Melville, turn round to this
side,

And I'll be the bridegroom, and you'll be the
bride."

Oh, 'twas a merry wedding, and the portion down
told,

Oh, bonnie Jeanie Melville, who was scarce sixteen years old.*

XIV.

DICKIE MACPHALION.

I WENT to the mill, but the miller was gone,
I sat me down, and cried ochone !
To think on the days that are past and gone
Of Dickie Macphalion that's slain.
  Shoo, shoo, shoolaroo,
To think on the days that are past and gone,
Of Dickie Macphalion that's slain.

---

* This ballad was first printed in "The Scottish Minstrel," vol. iv., 1822. The version there given differs con-
siderably from this. An "expurgated" text was printed
in "The Popular Rhymes of Scotland" in 1826, and,
mirabile dictu, is there said to be "printed for the *first*
time."

I sold my rock, I sold my reel,
And sae hae I my spinning wheel,
And a' to buy a cap of steel
For Dickie Macphalion that's slain !
   Shoo, shoo, shoolaroo,
And a' to buy a cap of steel
For Dickie Macphalion that's slain.*

XV.
GLASGOW PEGGIE.

As I cam' in by Glasgow town,
The Highland troops were a' before me,
And the bonniest lass that e'er I saw,
She lives in Glasgow, they ca' her Peggie.

I wad gie my bonnie black horse,
So wad I my gude grey naigie,
If I were twa hundred miles in the north,
And nane wi' me but my bonnie Peggie ! "

Up then spak' her father dear,
Dear wow ! but he was wondrous sorrie—
" Weel may ye steal a cow or a yowe,
But ye dare nae steal my bonnie Peggie."

Up then spak her mother dear,
Dear wow ! but she spak' wondrous sorrie—
" Now since I have brought ye up this length,
Wad ye gang awa' wi' a Highland fellow ? "

---

* A Ballad of evidently Irish origin.

He set her on his bonnie black horse,
He set himself on ,his gude grey naigie ;
And they have ridden o'er hills and dales,
And he's awa' wi' his bonnie Peggie.

They have ridden o'er hills and dales,
They have ridden o'er mountains many,
Until they cam' to a low, low glen,
And there he's lain down wi' his bonnie Peggie.

Up then spak' the Earl of Argyle,
Dear wow ! but he spak' wondrous sorrie—
"The bonniest lass in a' Scotland,
Is off and awa' wi' a Highland fellow."

Their bed was of the bonnie green grass,
Their blankets war o' the hay sae bonnie ;
He folded his philabeg below her head,
And he's lain down wi' his bonnie Peggie.

Up then spak' the bonnie Lowland lass,
And wow ! but she spak wondrous sorrie—
"I'se warrant my mither wad [hae a gay sair
    heart
To see me lien' here wi' you, my Willie."

" In my father's house there's feather beds,
Feather beds, and blankets mony ;
They're a' mine, and they'll sune be thine,
And what needs your mither be sae sorrie,
    Peggie?

"Dinna you see yon nine score o' kye,
Feeding on yon hill sae bonnie?
There a' mine, and they'll sune be thine,
And what needs your mither be sorrie, Peggie?

"Dinna ye see yon nine score o' sheep,
Feeding on yon brae sae bonnie?
They're a' mine, and they'll sune be thine,
And what needs your mither be sorrie for ye?

"Dinna ye see yon bonnie white house,
Shining on yon brae sae bonnie?
And I am the Earl of the Isle of Skye,
And surely my Peggie will be ca'd a lady."*

XVI.

TAM O' THE LIN.

TAM O' LIN's daughter scho sat on the stair,
And, "Wow," quo scho, "Father, am na I fair?
There's mony ane wed wi 'an unwhiter skin"—
"The deil whorl 't off," quo Tam o' the Lin.

Tam o' Lin's daughter scho sat on the brig,
And, "Wow," quo scho, "Father, am na I trig?"
The brig it brak', and she tummel'd in—
"Your tocher's paid," quo Tam o' the Lin.

---

* This ballad is better known under the title of the "Ear of Hume," or the "Banks of Omey."

XVII.

MAY COLLIN.

Oh, heard ye of a bloody knight.
  Lived in the south country ?
For he has betrayed eight ladies fair,
  And drowned them in the sea.

Then next he went to May Collin,
  She was her father's heir ;
The greatest beauty in the land,
  I solemnly declare.

"I am a knight of wealth and might,
  Of townlands twenty-three ;
And you'll be the lady of them all
  If you will go with me."

"Excuse me, then, Sir John," she says,
  "To wed I am too young—
Without I have my parents' leave,
  With you I darena gang."

"Your parents' leave you soon shall have,
  In that they will agree ;
For I have made a solemn vow
  This night you'll go with me."

From below his arm he pulled a charm,
  And stuck it in her sleeve ;
And he has made her go with him,
  Without her parents' leave.

Of gold and silver she has got
  With her twelve hundred pound ;
And the swiftest steed her father had
  She has ta'en to ride upon.

So privily they went along,
  They made no stop or stay,
Till they came to the fatal place,
  That they call Bunion Bay,

It being in a lonely place,
  And no house there was nigh,
The fatal rocks were long and steep,
  And none could hear her cry.

"Light down," he said, "fair May Collin,
  Light down, and speak with me,
For here I've drowned eight ladies fair,
  And the ninth one you shall be."

"Is this your bowers and lofty towers,
  So beautiful and gay,
Or is it for my gold," she said,
  "You take my life away ?"

" Strip off," he says, " thy jewels fine,
  So costly and so brave,
For they are too costly and too fine
  To throw in the sea wave."

" Take all I have my life to save,
  Oh, good Sir John, I pray,
Let it ne'er be said you killed a maid,
  Upon her wedding-day."

" Strip off," he says, " thy holland smock,
  " That's bordered with the lawn,
For it's too costly and too fine
  To rot on the sea sand."

" Oh, turn about, Sir John," she said,
  Your back about to me ;
For it never was comely for a man
  A naked woman to see."

But as he turned him round about,
  She threw him in the sea,
Saying, " Lie you there, you false Sir John,
  Where you thought to lay me.

"Oh, lie you there, you traitor false,
  Where you thought to lay me ;
For though you stripped me to the skin,
  Your clothes you've got with thee."

Her jewels fine she did put on,
    So costly, rich, and brave,
And then with speed she mounts his steed,
    So well she did behave.

That lady fair being void of fear,
    Her steed being swift and free,
And she has reached her father's gate
    Before the clock struck three.

Then first she called her stable groom,
    He was her waiting man ;
Soon as he heard his lady's voice,
    He stood with cap in hand.

" Where have you been, fair May Collin ?
    Who owns this dapple grey ? "
" It is a found one," she replied,
    " That I got on the way."

Then out bespoke the wily parrot
    Unto fair May Collin,
" What have you done with false Sir John,
    That went with you yestreen ? "

" Oh, hold your tongue, my pretty parrot,
    And talk no more of me ;
And where you had a meal a day,
    Oh, now you shall have three."

Then up bespoke her father dear,
  From his chamber where he lay,
" What aileth thee, my pretty Poll,
  That you chat so long ere day ? "

" The cat she came to my cage door,
  The thief I could not see,
And I called to fair May Collin
  To take the cat from me."

Then first she told her father dear
  The deed that she had done,
And next she told her mother dear,
  Concerning false Sir John.

" If this be true, fair May Collin,
  That you have told to me,
Before I either eat or drink,
  This false Sir John I'll see."

Away they went with one consent,
  At dawning of the day ;
Until they came to Carline Sands,
  And there his body lay :

His body tall, by that great fall,
  By the waves tossed to and fro,
The diamond ring that he had on,
  Was broke in pieces two.

And they have taken up his corpse
　To yonder pleasant green,
And there they have buried false Sir John,
　For fear he should be seen. *

---

* This is a much fuller set of the ballad than I ever saw
printed. It is probable that Collin, cr Colvin, is a corrup-
tion of Colvill ; and that Carline Sands means Carlinseugh
Sands, on the coast of Forfarshire. Sir John's charm
resembles that used by Sir John Colquhoun in 1633, and
the glamour of Faa, the Egyptian, touching whose amorous
adventure and tragical end, I may here mention some
lines expressive of the powers of the husband's family
which I found among the Macfarlane MSS. :—

　　" 'Twixt Wigton and the town of Air,
　　　Portpatrick and the cruives of Crea,
　　No man needs think for to bide there,
　　　Unless he court with Kennedie."

I will only add that May Collin's appropriation of her
lover's steed, though unromantic, may be justified by the
example of the Princess of Cathay herself, and Ariosto informs us that Angelica was never at a loss for a palfrey ;
when Orlando had seized one, from which she fell, she
would steal another.—C. K. S.

The ballad was first published in Mr. Herd's "Ancient
and Modern Scottish Songs " (1769). A third version is
given by Motherwell.

XVIII.

MY MITHER BUILT A WEE, WEE HOUSE.

(*Tune*, " Birks of Abergeldie."*)

My mither built a wee, wee house,
A wee, wee house, a wee, wee house,
My mither built a wee, wee house,
To keep me frae the men, O !
The wa's fell in, and I fell out,
The wa's fell in, and I fell out,
The wa's fell in, and I fell out,
Amang the merry men, O !

How can I keep my maidenhead,
My maidenhead, my maidenhead,
How can I keep my maidenhead,
Amang sae mony men, O ?
Ane auld mouldy maidenhead,
Ane auld mouldy maidenhead,
Ane auld mouldy maidenhead,
Seven years and ten, O !

The captain bad a guinea for 't,
A guinea for 't, a guinea for 't,
The captain bad a guinea for 't,
The colonel he bad ten, O !
The sergeant he bad naething for 't,
Bad naething for 't, bad naething for 't
The sergeant he bad naething for 't.
And he came farrest ben, O !

---

* *Sic* in original, but "The Birks of *Aberfeldie* " is the
name the tune is best known by.

XIX.

THE TWA BROTHERS.

THERE were twa brethern in the north,
They went to the school* thegither ;
The one unto the other said,
" Will you try a warsle afore ? "

They warsled up, they warsled down,
Till Sir John fell to the ground,
And there was a knife in Sir Willie's pouch,
Gied him a deadlie wound.

" Oh, brither, dear, take me on your back,
Carry me to yon burn clear,
And wash the blood from off my wound,
And it will bleed nae mair."

He took him up upon his back,
Carried him to yon burn clear,
And wash'd the blood from off his wound,
But aye it bled the mair.

" Oh brither, dear, take me on your back,
Carry me to yon kirk-yard ;
And dig a grave baith wide and deep,
And lay my body there."

---

* Chase is sometimes substituted for school.—C. K. S.

He's ta'en him up upon his back,
Carried him to yon kirk-yard ;
And dug a grave baith deep and wide,
And laid his body there.

"But what will I say to my father dear,
Gin he chance to say, ' Willie, whar's John?'"
"Oh, say that he's to England gone,
To buy him a cask of wine."

"And what will I say to my mother dear,
Gin she chance to say, ' Willie, whar's John?'"
"Oh, say that he's to England gone,
To buy her a new silk gown."

"An what will I say to my sister dear,
Gin she chance to say, ' Willie, whar's John?'"
"Oh, say that he's to England gone,
To buy her a wedding-ring."

"But what will I say to her you lo'e dear,
Gin she cry, ' Why tarries my John?'"
"Oh, tell her I lie in kirk-land fair,
And home again will never come."*

---

* In the month of July, 1588, at the Drum, near Dal-
keith, William, Master of Somerville, accidentally killed his
brother John, with whom he had ever lived in the most
affectionate manner, by the unexpected discharge of his
pistol ("Memorie of the Somervilles," vol. i. p. 466). This
event, I am convinced, is the origin of this ballad, of which
a fuller and more correct edition is to be found in Jamieson.
As to kirk-land, my copy has only kirk-yard, till the last
verse, where *land* has been added from conjecture. Kirk-

XX.

THE TWA LASSES.

O BESSIE BELL and Mary Gray,
    They war twa bonnie lasses !
They bigget a bower on yon burn brae,
    And theekit it o'er wi' rashes.
They theekit it o'er wi' rashes green,
    They theekit it o'er with heather,
But the pest cam' frae the burrows town,
    And slew them baith thegither !

They thought to lye in Methven Kirk yard,
    Amang their noble kin,
But they maun lye in Stronach Haugh,
    To biek forenent the sin.
And Bessie Bell and Mary Gray,
    They war twa bonnie lasses !
They biggit a bower on yon burn brae,
    And theekit it o'er wi' rashes.*

END OF PART I.

---

land, or Inchmurry, is in Perthshire.—N.B. A similar
accident happened in the Stair family, 1682.—C. K. S.

This ballad was first published by Jamieson in his
"Popular Ballads and Songs" (1806). A third version is
given by Motherwell.

* Bessy Bell and Mary Gray died of the plague, com-
municated by their lover, in the year 1645. Their romantic
history may be found in "Pennant's Tour," and in the
"Statistical Account of Scotland." The more modern words
of this ballad were composed by Allan Ramsay.—C. K. S.

A

BALLAD BOOK.

A

Bibliotheca Curiosa.

A

BALLAD BOOK;

OR,

POPULAR AND ROMANTIC BALLADS AND
SONGS CURRENT IN ANNANDALE AND
OTHER PARTS OF SCOTLAND.

COLLECTED BY

CHARLES KIRKPATRICK SHARPE.

Reprinted from the Rare Original Edition of 1824,

and Edited by

EDMUND GOLDSMID, F.R.H.S.

PART II.

PRIVATELY PRINTED, EDINBURGH.

1883.

This Edition is limited to seventy-five Large Paper copies, and two hundred and seventy-five Small Paper copies, issued only to Subscribers.

.

UNWIN BROTHERS, PRINTERS, LONDON AND CHILWORTH.

INDEX TO PART II.

A BALLAD BOOK.

XXI.

THE BONNY HOUSE OF AIRLIE.

IT fell on a day, and a bonny simmer day,
  When green grew aits and barley,
That there fell out a great dispute
  Between Argyll and Airlie.

Argyll has raised an hundred men,
  An hunder harness'd rarely,
And he's awa' by the back of Dunkell,
  To plunder the Castle of Airlie.

Lady Ogilvie looks o'er her bower window
  And oh, but she looks weary ;
And there she spy'd the great Argyll,
  Come to plunder the bonny House of Airlie.

" Come down, come down, my Lady Ogilvie,
　　Come down, and kiss me fairly."
" O, I winna kiss the fause Argyll,
　　If he should　na leave a standing stane in
　　　Airlie."

He hath taken her by the left shoulder,
　　Says, " Dame, where lies thy dowry ? "
" Oh, it's east and west yon wan water side,
　　And its down by the banks of the Airlie."

They hae sought it up, they hae sought it down,
　　They hae sought it maist severely ;
Till they fand it in the fair plumb tree,
　　That shines on the bowling-green of Airlie.

He hath taken her by the middle sae small,
　　And, O, but she grat sairly :
And laid her down by the bonny burn-side,
　　Till they plundered the Castle of Airlie.

" Gif my gude lord war here this night,
　　As he is with King Charlie,
Neither you nor ony ither Scottish lord,
　　Durst awow to the plundering of, Airlie.

" Gif-my gude lord war now at hame,
　　As he is with his King,
There durst nae a Campbell in a 'Argyll,
　　Set fit on Airlie green.

"Ten bonny sons I have born unto him,
The eleventh ne'er saw his daddy,
But though I had an hundred mair,
I'd gie them a' to King Charlie."*

XXII.

O, GIN YE WAR DEAD, GUDEMAN.

O, GIN ye war dead, Gudeman,
And a green sod on your heid, Gudeman;
Then I wad war my widowhood,
Upon a rantin' Highlandman !
There's a sheep's heid in the pat, Gudeman,
A sheep's heid in the pat, Gudeman,
The broo to me, the horns to thee,
An' the flesh to our John Highlandman.

Chorus.

Sing round about the fire wi' a rung scho ran,
An' round about the fire wi' a rung scho ran,
An' round about the fire wi' a rung scho ran,
"Had awa' your blue breeks frae me, Gude-
man."

---

* In the year 1640, Airlie Castle was destroyed by the Marquis of Argyll—a nobleman never accused of incontinence, as might be supposed from this ballad, which is erroneous in another point, at least ; no Lady Ogilvie had eleven sons : the first Earl's wife had three, his daughter-in-law, who is probably the heroine of the song, only one ; she herself was a daughter of Lord Banff.—C. K. S.

This ballad is very common in all parts of Scotland ; innumerable versions have appeared.

XXIII.

THE DREAM.

(*Tune :* " Gramachree.")
LAST night I dreamt my Peggy
    Was in beneath the bed ;
And up I got upo' my doup,
    And, oh ! but I was glad.

I pat my hand beneath the bed
    To tak' her be the lug,
But instead o' my dear Peggy,
    I gat the water mug ! *

XXIV.

THE CRAB.

OUR gude wife's wi' bairn, and that's of a lad,
And sho's ta'en a greenin' for a fish crab.
        With my hey jing, &c.

Up gat our gudeman, and cleekit to his claithes,
And he's awa' to the sea-side, trippin' on his taes.
        With my hey jing, &c.

---

* The above song used to be sung by a gentleman very
eminent at the Scottish Bar, who was born in the year
1680.—C. K. S.

"Have ye ony crab-fish?"—"One, two, three."
"Tippence is the price o' them gin you and I'll
agree."
>With my hey jing, &c.

He's pu'd out his purse, and bought the biggest
ane,
He's put it in his nicht mutch, and he's come
toddlin' hame.
>With my hey jing, &c.

He wadna put it on the dresser, for fylin' a' the
dishes,
But he pat it in the chalmer pat, where our gude
wife——.
>With my hey jing, &c.

Up gat the guid wife, an' for to mak' her dam,
Up gat the crab-fish, and took her be the wame.
>With my hey jing, &c.

Up gat the gudeman, to redd the fish's claws,
Up gat the crab-fish, and took him by the nose.
>With my hey jing, &c.*

---

* This gross old ditty is founded on a story in "Le
Moyen de Parvenir," a book of which the extreme wit is
at least equalled by its beastliness.—C. K. S.

XXV.

ANDREW CAR.

Chorus.

Hey for Andrew, Andrew,
Hey for Andrew Car !
He gaed to bed to the lass,
And forgot to bar the door !

Andrew Car is cunnin',
And Andrew Car is slee,
And Andrew Car is winnin',
And Andrew Car for me.
    Sing hey for Andrew, &c.

O it was Andrew Car,
O it was him, indeed ;
O it was Andrew Car
Wha gat my maidenhead.
    Sing hey for Andrew, &c,

XXVI.

THE HAGGIS O' DUNBAR.

Hey, the Haggis o' Dunbar,
  Fatharalinkum Feedle ;
Mony better, few waur,
  Fatharalinkum Feedle.

For to mak' this Haggis nice,
  Fatharalinkum Feedle ;
They pat in a peck o' lice,
  Fatharalinkum Feedle.

For to mak' this Haggis fat,
  Fatharalinkum Feedle ;
They put in a scabbit cat,
  Fatharalinkum Feedle.

   ✲   ✲   ✲   ✲   ✲

XXVII.
THE BONNY LAD.

HE's a bonny, bonny lad that's a courting me,
He's a bonny, bonny lad that's a courting me ;
He's cripple of a leg, and blind of an e'e,
He's a bonny, bonny lad that's a courting me !

   ✲   ✲   ✲   ✲   ✲

XXVIII.
FAIR MARGARET OF CRAIGNARGAT.

FAIR Margaret of Craignargat
  Was the flow'r of all her kin,
And she's fallen in love with a false young man,
  Her ruin to begin.

The more she lov'd, the more it prov'd
  Her fatal destiny ;
And he that sought her overthrow,
  Shar'd of her misery.

Before that lady she was born,
 Her mother, as we find,
She dreamt she had a daughter fair,
 That was both dumb and blind.

But as she sat in her bow'r door,
 A viewing of her charms,
There came a raven from the south,
 And pluck'd her from her arms.

Three times on end she dreamt this dream,
 Which troubled sore her mind,
That from that very night and hour,
 She could no comfort find.

Now she has sent for a wise woman,
 Liv'd nigh unto the port,
Who being call'd, instantly came,
 That lady to comfort.

To her she told her dreary dream,
 With salt tears in her eye ;
Hoping that she would read the same,
 Her mind to satisfy.

"Set not your heart on children young,
 Whate'er their fortune be,
And if I tell what shall befall,
 Lay not the blame on me.

" The raven which you dreamed of,
   He is a false young man,
With subtile heart and flatt'ring tongue,
   Your daughter to trepan.

" Both night and day, 'tis you I pray
   For to be on your guard,
For many are the subtile wyles,
   By which youth are ensnar'd."

When she had read the dreary dream,
   It vexed her more and more,
For Craignargat of birth and state,
   Liv'd nigh unto the shore.

But as in age her daughter wax'd,
   Her beauty did excel
All the ladies far and near,
   That in that land did dwell.

The Gordon, Hay, and brave Agnew,
   Three knights of high degree,
Unto the dame a courting came,
   All for her fair beauty.

Which of these men they asked her then,
   That should her husband be ?
But scornfully she did reply,
   " I'll wed none of the three."

" Since it is so, where shall we go,
  A match for thee to find ?
That art so fair and beautiful,
  That none can suit thy mind."

With scorn and pride she answer made,
  " You'll ne'er choice one for me,
Nor will I wed against my mind,
  For all their high degree."

The brave Agnew, whose heart was true,
  A solemn vow did make,
Never to love a woman more,
  All for that lady's sake.

To counsel this lady was deaf,
  To judgment she was blind,
Which griev'd her tender parents dear
  And troubled sore their mind,

From the Isle of Man a courter came,
  And a false young man was he,
With subtile heart and flatt'ring tongue,
  To court this fair lady.

This young man was a bold outlaw,
  A robber and a thief,
But soon he gain'd this lady's heart,
  Which caused all their grief.

"O, will you wed," her mother said,
 "A man you do not know,
For to break your parents' heart,
 With shame but and with woe?"

"Yes, I will go with him," she said,
 "Either by land or sea,
For he's the man I've pitched on,
 My husband for to be."

"O, let her go," her father said,
 "For she shall have her will.
My curse and mallison she's get,
 For to pursue her still."

"Your curse, father, I don't regard,
 Your blessing I'll ne'er crave;
To the man I love, I'll constant prove,
 And never him deceive."

On board with him fair Marg'ret's gone,
 In hopes his bride to be.
But mark you well, and I shall tell
 Of their sad destiny.

They had not sail'd a league but five,
 Till the storm began to rise;
The swelling seas ran mountains high,
 And dismal were the skies,

B

In deep despair, that lady fair,
 For help aloud she cries,
While crystal tears, like fountains ran
 Down from her lovely eyes.

"O ! I have got my father's curse,
 My pride for to subdue ;
With sorrows great my heart will break,
 Alas ! what shall I do ?

"O, were I at my father's house,
 His blessing to receive,
Then on my bended knees I'd fall
 His pardon for to crave.

" To aid my grief, there's no relief,
 To speak it is in vain,
Likewise my loving parents dear,
 I ne'er shall see again."

The wind and waves did both conspire,
 The lives for to devour,
That gallant ship that night was lost,
 And never was seen more.

When tidings to Craignargat came,
 Of their sad overthrow,
It griev'd her tender parents' heart,
 Afresh began their woe.

Of the dreary dream that she had seen,
   And often thought upon,
" O fatal news," her mother cries,
   "My darling, she is gone !

" O fair Marg'ret, ·I little thought,
   The seas should be thy grave,
When first thou left thy father's house,
   Without thy parents' leave."

May this tragedy a warning be,
   To children while they live,
That they may love their parents dear,
   Their blessing to receive.*

---

* Craignargat is a promontory in the bay of Luce. Although almost surrounded by the Barony of Mochrum, it was long possessed by a branch of the family of Macdowall, which was probably our heroine's surname. On the head of Fair Margaret's lovers, it may be remarked that the Agnews of Lochnaw are a very ancient family, and hereditary Sheriffs of Wigton. The Gordon mentioned was probably Gordon of Craighlaw, whose castle was situated about five miles from Craignargat, in the parish of Kirkcowan, considered so remote before the formation of military roads, that the local proverb says, "Out of the world and into Kirkcowan." The Hays of Park dwelt on the coast, about six miles from Craignargat ; but it is singular that the lady is not complimented with a Dunbar as her lover, the Place of Mochrum, as the old tower is called, being only two miles from her reputed residence.—C. K. S.

This ballad, according to Motherwell, was a common stall ballad, about 1760.

XXIX.

KEMPY KAYE.

KEMPY KAYE'S a wooing gane,
　　Far, far ayont the sea,
An' he has met with an auld auld man,
　　His gudefather to be.

" Gae scrape yeersel, and gae scart yeersel,
　　And mak your bruchty face clean,
For the wooers are to be here the nicht,
　　And yeer body's to be seen.*

" What's the matter wi' you, my fair maiden,
　　You look so pale and wan ?
I'm sure you was once the fairest maiden,
　　That ever the sun shined on."

Sae they scrapit her, and they scartit her,
　　Like the face of any assy pan ;
And in cam Kempy Kaye himself,
　　A clever and tall young man.

His teeth they were like tether sticks,
　　His nose was three feet lang ;
Between his shouthers was ells three,
　　Between his een a span.

---

* Var. Kempy Kaye's to be here the nicht,
　　　　Or else the morn at een.—C. K. S.

" I'm coming to court your dochter dear,
 An' some pairt of your gear."
An' by my sooth," quo' Bengoleer,
 " She'll sair a man o' weir."

" My dochter she's a thrifty lass,
 She span seven year to me,
An' if it war weil counted up,
 Full ten wobs it would be."

He led his dochter by the han,
 His dochter ben brought he ;
" O, is not she the fairest lass,
 That's in great Christendye ? "

Ilka hair intil her head,
 Was like a heather cow,
And ilka louse aninder it,
 Was like a lintseed bow.*

She had lauchty teeth an' kaily lips,
 An' wide lugs fu' o' hair ;
Her pouches fu' o' pease meal daigh,
 War hinging down her spare.

Ilka ee intil her head,
 Was like a rotten ploom,
An' down down browit was the quean,
 An' sairly did she gloom.

---

* Var. Was like a brucket yowe.

Ilka nail upon her hand,
  Was like an iron rake,
An' ilka teeth into her head,
  Was like a tether stake.

She gied to him a gay gravat,
  O' the auld horse's sheet,
And he gied her a gay gold ring,
  O' the auld couple reet.*

XXX.

THE PUDDY AND THE MOUSE.

THERE lived a puddy in a well,
And a merry mouse in a mill.

Puddy he'd a wooin' ride,
Sword and pistol by his side.

---

* *i.e.* root.—C. K. S.

This song my learned readers will perceive to be of Scandinavian origin ; and that the wooer's name was probably suggested by Sir Kayes of the Round Table, whose lady failed to prove her chastity in the troublesome affair of the mantle. The description of Bengoleer's daughter resembles that of the enchanted damsel who appeared to courteous King Henrie.

N.B.—This and the following ballad should have been placed much earlier in the series.—C. K. S.

Puddy cam to the mouse's wonne,
" Mistress Mouse, are you within ? "

"Yes, kind sir, I am within,
Saftly do I sit and spin."

" Madame, I am come to woo,
Marriage I must have of you.''

" Marriage I will grant you nane,
Till Uncle Rotten he comes hame."

" Uncle Rotten's now come hame,
Fye gar busk the bride alang."

Lord Rotten sat at the head o' the table,
Because he was baith stout and able.

Wha is't that sits next the wa',
But Lady Mouse baith jimp and sma' ?

Wha is't that sits next the bride,
But the sola puddy wi' his yellow side ?*

Syme cam the dewk but and the drake,
The dewk took the puddy and gart him squaik.

---

* Var. Wha sat at the table fit,
Wha but froggy and his lame fit ?—C. K. S.

Than cam in the carle cat,
Wi' a fiddle on his back ;
" Want ye ony music here ? "＊

The puddy he swam down the brook,
The drake he catch'd him in his fluke.

The cat he pu'd Lord Rotten down,
The kittlens they did claw his crown.

But Lady Mouse baith jimp and sma',
Crept into a hole beneath the wa';
" Squeak," quo' she, " I'm weel awa'."†

＊ Var. Then in cam the gude grey cat,
     Wi' a' the kittlens at her back.—C. K. S.

† Among the songs enumerated in the " Complainte of
Scotland " (1594) is, " The frog cam to the myl dur," probably founded on the same legend with this, which has a
chorus, " Cuddie alone and I," &c., not worthy of insertion.
In November, 1580, the Stationers licensed to E. White
" A ballad of a most strange wedding of the frogge and the
mouse," which has since frequently appeared in a more
modern shape. See also in D'Urffey's Pills, vol. v., " A
ditty on a high amour at St. James's ; the words by Mr.
D'Urffey, and set to a comical tune."—C. K. S.

XXXI.
THE EARL OF ERROL.

O ERROL it's a bonny place,
  It stands in yonder glen ;
The lady lost the rights of it,
  The first night she gaed hame.

Chorus.

A waly, and a waly,
  According as ye ken ;
The thing we ca' the ranting o't
  Our Lady lies her lane, O !

" What need I wash my apron,
  Or hing it on yon door,
What need I truce my petticoat,
  It hangs even down before ? "
    A waly, &c.

Errol's up to Edinburgh gaen,
  That bonny burrows town !
He has chused the Barber's daughter,
  The toss of a' that town.
    A waly, &c.

He's ta'en her by the milk-white hand,
  He's led her o'er the green,
And twenty times he kist her,
  Before his Lady's een.
    A waly, &c.

" Look up, look up, now Peggy,
　　Look up and think nae shame,
　For I'll give thee five hundred pound,
　　To buy to thee a gown ! "
　　　A waly, &c.

" Look up, look up, now Peggy,
　　Look up and think nae shame ;
　For I'll gie thee five hundred pound,
　　To bear to me a son."
　　　A waly, &c.

" Your name is Kate Carnegie,
　　And I'm Sir Gilbert Hay ;
　I'll gar your father sell his lands,
　　Your tocher gude to pay."
　　　A waly, &c.

Now he may take her back again,
　　Do wi' her what he can,
　For Errol canna please her,
　　Nor ane o' a' his men.
　　　A waly, &c.

" Go fetch to me a pint of wine,
　　Go fill it to the brim ;
　That I may drink my gude Lord's health,
　　Tho' Errol be his name."
　　　A waly, &c.

She has ta'en the glass into her hand,
    She has putten poison in ;
She has sign'd it to her dorty lips,
    But ne'er a drop went in.
        A waly, &c.

Up then spak a little page,
    He was o' Errol's kin,
" Now fie upon ye, lady gay,
    There's poison there within."
        A waly, &c.

" It's hold your hand now, Kate," he says,
    " Hold it back again,
For Errol shall not drink on't,
    Nor none of all his men."
        A waly, &c.

She has taen the sheets into her arms,
    She has thrown them o'er the wa';
" Since I maun gae maiden hame again,
    Awa', Errol, awa'."
        A waly, &c.

She's down the back o' the garden,
    And O ! as she did murne !
" How can a warkman crave his wage,
    When he never wrought a turn ? "

A waly and á waly,
According as ye ken ;
The thing we ca' the ranting o't,
Our Lady lies her lane, O !*

XXIII.
RICHIE STORIE.

THE Earl o' Wigton had three daughters,
O braw wallie ! but they were bonnie ;
The youngest o' them, and the bonniest too,
Has fallen in love wi' Richie Storie.

---

*The following extract from a letter addressed by Keith, of
Benholm, to Captain Brown, at Paris, explains the subject of
this ballad, which was preserved by the peasantry of Annandale, probably owing to the circumstance of Lord Southesque,
Lady Errol's brother, being at one time possessor of Hod-
dam Castle : " You may have heard ere this of Glencairne's
marriage with the Countess Dowager of Tweddell, mother-
in-lawe to your cousin ; and what accessione of French
landes Glencairne's son is lyke to bring to his familie, by
a cadet of their hous and name, a French marquis, who
hath carried my Lord Kilmaurs and his brother to France
for that effect. Then the death of your cousin's lady, my
Lady Wigtoune ; with that of the Erll of Annandell, Bau-
vaird by his death becoming Viscount Stormont and Lord
Scoon. Lastly, the sadd (and not lyke heard of in this land
amongst eminent persons) story of the Erll of Erroll's im-
potencie, which is lyke, being cum to publick hearing, to
draw deeper betwix him and Southesk, than is alledgit it
hath done 'twixt him and Southesk's daughter. These are
the meane emergents we are taken up with, whilst beyond sea
empyres are overturning. Scoone, 22d. Feb., 1659."—C.KS.

See also a version in Maidment's " North Countrie
Garland."

" Here's a letter for ye, madame,
Here's a letter for ye, madame,
The Erle o' Home wad fain presume,
To be a suitor to ye, madame."

"I'l hae nane o' your letters, Richie,
I'l hae nane o' your letters, Richie,
For I've made a vow, and I'l keep it true,
That I'l have none but you, Ritchie."

"O do not say so, madame,
O do not say so, madame,
For I have neither land nor rent,
For to maintain you o', madame.

"Ribands ye maun wear, madame,
Ribands ye maun wear, madame,
With the bands about your neck,
O' the goud that shines sae clear, madame."

" I'l lie ayont a dyke, Richie,
I'l lie ayont a dyke, Richie,
And I'l be aye at your command,
And bidding whan ye like, Richie."

O, he's gane on the braid, braid road,
And she's gane through the broom sae bonnie,
Her siiken robes down to her heels,
And she's awa' wi' Richie Storie.

This lady gade up the Parliament stair,
Wi' pendles in her lugs sae bonnie,
Mony a lord lifted his hat,
But little did they ken she was Richie's lady.

Up then spak the Erle o' Home's lady,
" Was na ye richt sorrie, Annie,
To leave the lands o' bonnie Cumbernauld,
And follow Richie Storie, Annie ? "

" O, what need I be sorrie, madame,
O, what need I be sorrie, madame,
For I've got them that I like best,
And war ordained for me, madame ! "

"Cumbernauld is mine, Annie,
Cumbernauld is mine, Annie,
And a' that's mine, it shall be thine,
As we sit at the wine, Annie."*

---

* John, third Earl of Wigtown, had six sons and three
daughters. The second, Lady Lillias Fleming, was so in-
discreet as to marry a footman, by whom she had issue.
She and her husband assigned her provision to Lieutenant-
Colonel John Fleming, who discharged her renunciation,
dated in October, 1673.—C. K. S.

This ballad was sung to the tune of "Braw lads o' Gala
Water."

XXXIII.

THE RAPE OF ARNGOSK. (A Fragment.)*

THE Highlandmen hae a' come down,
They've a come down almost,
They've stowen away the bonnie lass,
The Lady of Arngosk.

* This fragment I cannot illustrate, either from history or
tradition. Sir William Murray, third son of Sir William
Murray of Tullibardine, married Margaret Barclay, the
heiress of Arngosk and Kippo, in the reign of King James
IV.; but it is very unlikely that the ballad alludes to that
match, particularly as it is remembered to have concluded
with the lady's restoration to her friends, a *finale* not un-
common in such cases, with which, by the way, our Scottish
annals abound.—Ex. grat. A.D. 1336, Allan of Winton
forcibly carried off the young heiress of Seton ; this pro-
duced a feud in Lothian, some favouring the ravisher, while
others sought to bring him to punishment. Fordun says,
that on this occasion an hundred ploughs in Lothian were
laid aside from labour. Master Bowy, in his very curious
MS. History of the House of Glenurquhay, informs us
that "John Mackrom Macalaster M'Gregor, in anno ——,
ravischit Helene Campbell, dochtir to Sir Colene Campbell
of Glenurquhay, Knicht. This Helene Campbell was
widow, and Lady of Lochbuy, and she was ravischit. The
foresaid John was not richteous air to the M'Gregor, but was
principal of the clan Donlogneir." Sir Colin, "wha
departit this lyfe in the Tour of Straphillane, 24th Sept.,
1480," understanding that his daughter had become recon-
ciled to her forced marriage, waylaid his son-in-law at the
hill of Drummond, slew him, and cutting off his head, put
it into a basket, and covered it with apples. This, as an
acceptable present, he sent to his daughter by a messenger,
charged not to mention what was concealed at the bottom.
In the pedigree of the clan Gregor, it is said that Malcolm
M'Gregor *married the lady with a view to conciliate the*

Behind her back they've tied her hands,
An' then they set her on—
"I winna gang wi' you," she said,
"Nor ony Highland loon."

*　　*　　*　　*　　*　　*

differences between the two families, and that she composed
a mournful song upon his death, which is still preserved :
probably the very ditty now attributed to Rob Roy's widow.
Bothwell's violence to Queen Marie is well known.   In the
year 1591, Lord Fountainhall notes from the Criminal
Records of Edinburgh, "Dame Jean Ramsay, Lady
Warriston (she was of the house of Dalheusy), and Advo-
cate, *contra* Robert Carncroce. called Meikle Rob, and
others, for ravishing of her in March last, contrare to the
Acts of Parliament."   1594, "the 14th of August, Christian
Johnstoun, ane widow in Edinburgh, revest be Patrick
Aikenhead.   The towne wes put in ane grate fray be the
ringing of the common bell ; the said Christiane was
followit and brocht back fra him, sua that the said Patrick
got no advantage of her."—*Birrell's Diary.*   In the year
1680, Patrick Carnegie, son to the Earl of Northesk, carried
off by force from the house of Pilcoye, Mary Gray, heiress
of Ballegerno, a child not quite eleven years of age.   She
was recovered by her friends fifteen days after.   The last
case I shall mention is from Fountainhall : "January 7th,
1638, James Boswell, in Kinghorn, brother to Balmuto, is
pursued by Anna Carmichael, for ravishing her out of her
father's house, and wounding her father, and carrying her
to the Queensferry, where she was rescued ; and being
absent, he is declared fugitive, whereon his escheat falls.',
It may be added that in Fountainhall's MS. is the following
curious notice concerning Lord Stormont, descended from
the heiress of Arngosk : "About this tyme (June, 1668) was
given in a bill to the Lords of Secret Counsell complaining
on my Lord Stormond for fraudulent abstracting of Gibson,
the Laird of Durie's niece, to whom the custodie of her
person in law belongeth ; and for being art and part thereof,

XXXIV.
MALCOLM OF BALBEDIE.

BALBEDIE has a second son,
   They ca' him Michael Malcolm,
He gangs about Balgonie dykes,
   Huntin' and hawkin' ;
  He's stowen awa' the bonnie lass,
   An' kept the widow wakin'.*

XXXV.
I HAVE BEEN AT NEWBURN.

I HAVE been at Newburn, I was in the tower,
I have been in Scotland with a royal power,
I have been with Gilbert, and Marg'ret Kennedy,
But such a huffing parliament did I never see !

Thou shalt get a night-cap and a mourning ring,
And to kepp thy head, thy friends a cloth shall
   bring,
And in a wooden casement thy head shall be
   bound,
But thy lusty corpse must stink above the ground.

by accession either antecedent, concomitant, or subsequent.
This bill was given in by Durie, and after a long
dispute, the wholle resulting on my Lord Stormond's oath,
he denied all accession thereto, though it was strongly
soupçouned he was not free."—C. K. S.

  * Malcolm of Balbedie appears to have been a cadet of
the Lochor family, whose representative was created a
Baronet of Nova Scotia in the year 1665. I do not know
the anecdote on which this fragment was composed.—
C.K.S.

Thou shalt be conducted from Thames to Tweed-
    side,
Like a malefactor thy feet shall be tyed,
And from that scurvy process the lawyers shall
    be free,
Thou thought to catch these men, but we have
    catcht thee.*

XXXVI.
TO LAUDERDALE.

LAUDERDALE, what has become
    Of all thy former huffing,
IIas the Commons struck thee dumb,
    And sent thee thus a snuffing? .
Or is it that the late address
For removing thee and Bess,
            Does vex thee? &c.

Since the kingdoms thou must quit,
    And seek new habitation,
Will not thy proud Grace think fit
    T' erect a new plantation?
And since thou now begins to reel,
Pray thee go to Old Brazile,
            And lord it, &c.

---

* This and the following song allude to some political
misfortunes of the Duke of Lauderdale, in the year 1675,
which are well known to every reader of history. Gilbert
is Dr. Burnet, and Margaret, Lady Margaret Kennedy,
his wife.—C.K.S.

XXXVII.

ANNIE LAURIE.

MAXWELTON banks are bonnie,
Whare early fa's the dew ;
Whare me and Annie Laurie
Made up the promise true ;
Made up the promise true,
And never forget will I,
And for bonnie Annie Laurie
I'd lay down my head and die.

She's backit like a peacock,
She's breastit like a swan,
She's jimp about the middle,
Her waist ye weill may span ;
Her waist you weil may span,
And she has a rolling eye,
And for bonnie Annie Laurie
I'd lay down my head end die.*

---

* Sir Robert Laurie, first baronet of the Maxwelton
family (created 27th March, 1685), by his second wife, a
daughter of Riddell of Minto, had three sons and four
daughters, of whom Annie was much celebrated for her
beauty, and made a conquest of Mr. Douglas of Fingland,
who is said to have composed these verses—under an
unlucky star, for the lady afterwards married Mr.
Ferguson of Craigderroch.

XXXVIII.

FY, FY, MARG'RET.

(*Tune :* " How are ye, Kimmer ? ")

" Fy, fy, Marg'ret are ye in?
I nae sooner heard it than I did rin,
Down the gate to tell ye, down the gate to tell
 ye,
Down the gate to tell ye, we'll no be left the skin.

Weel might I kent a' was nae richt,
For I dreamt o' red and green a' the last nicht ;
And twa cats fechtin, and twa cats fechtin,
And twa cats fechtin, I waken'd wi' the fricht.

Fare ye weel, woman, I maun rin,
Trew ye, gif our neighbour Eppie be in,
And auld Robie Barber, and auld Robbie Barber,
And auld Robbie Barber, for I maun tell him.

" Bide a wee, woman, and gies't a' out—
They're bringing in black Papary, I doubt, I
 doubt,
And sad reformation, sad reformation,
Sad reformation in a' the kirks about.

Mickle do they say, and mair do we hear,
The Frenches and the Irishes are a' coming here,
And we'll be a' murder'd, murder'd, murder'd,
We'll a' be murder'd, before the new year."

XXXIX.

A Ballad, Being the True Case of Mrs. Elspet, a Lady's Gentlewoman, near Edinburgh.

LANG hae I lo'ed the blate Mass John,
  And sair my breast has smarted ;
I never saw a Dominie
  Was half sae cruel-hearted !

With pleasing words I feast his ears,
  With dainty food I fill him ;
I would not take the Chamberlain,
  But that did naething till him !

When he was with the toothache fash'd,
  I bled his gums with leeches ;
To keep him warm, I sewed mysel',
  Three buttons on his breeches,

I lo'e him in a lawful way,
  No lawful love is wicked ;
I ne'er set on the succar pan,
  But he got aye a lick o't.

Whene'er my dearie would came in,
  The door was never lockit ;
Nor wanted he for a la creesh,
  And seed-cake in his pocket.

I cut the phlegm with Athole brose,
    When cauld did quite confound him ;
I gave him wangrace in his bed,
    And row'd the blankets round him.

With darning his auld coarsest sarks,
    I scarce have left a thumb on ;
But sae I should, for chaplains used
    To love the gentlewoman.

But tho' he reads the Bible book,
    It makes but sma' impression ;
Indeed, he catch'd the cook with Kate,
    And sent them to the Session.

They did not well in what they did,
    So ill the matter ended ;
But lawful love's another thing,
    And ought to be commended.

With comfort met we should delight,
    Mankind should not miscarry ;
But he, for all that I can do,
    Will neither burn nor marry.

Hoot, fye for shame—be brisk, Mass John,
    Ye look as ye were sleepin' ;
Ye craw not like a stately fowl,
    But cackle like a capon.

Oh, dour, Mass John—oh, dreigh, Mass John,
  When I have told you sae far !
A shame light on your loggerhead,
  Ye doited, donnart, duffar ! *

XL.

THE DISTRAUGHT GUDE WIFE.

(*Tune :* " O London is a Fine Town.")

WAS ever dame in such distress ?
  My heart is full of care ;
Such various plagues torment my mind,
  That I am in despair.

I'm on and off, and off and on,
  And know not what to do ;
I have a cook to dress my meat,
  But I want to get me two.

This cook a handy damsel is,
  And dresses very weel,
Her kitchen is as clean's her face,
  And her pewther shines like steel.

---

* This and the following ballad were written by Charles Lord Binning, who died in the lifetime of his father, the Earl of Haddington, 1733. (See Park's edition of Walpole's " Royal and Noble Authors, vol. v.)

But she has no experience,
　And has so little seen,
That when I want variety,
　She kills me with the spleen.

I have a man cook in my view,
　To help her out a dish,
That when she is employ'd with meat,
　The lad may dress the fish.

But then the lad a head cook is,
　And second will not be ;
I must pack off the lass, I fear,
　For I can't afford her fee.

But then the lass has done no fault —
　I'll keep her, I'm resolved —
I'll get the man to give her half,
　And so the doubt is solv'd.

But what if they should not agree —
　They will my victuals spoil ;
He'll say 'tis her, and she 'tis him,
　And plague me with turmoil.

I'll not have him, and part with her,
　And yet I'll have him too ;
I'll part with her—no, no, I won't —
　O stars, what shall I do?

XLI.

COLD SIR PETER.

OH, wherefor did I cross the Forth,
　　And leave my love behind me,
Why did I venture to the north,
　　With one that does not mind me?

Had I but visited Carin!
　　It would have been much better,
Than pique the prudes, and make a din,
　　For careless, cold, Sir Peter!

I'm sure I've seen a better limb,
　　And twenty better faces;
But still my mind it ran on him,
　　When I was at the races.

At night when we went to the ball,
　　Were many there discreeter;
The well-bred Duke,* and lively Maule,
　　Panmure behav'd much better.

They kindly show'd their courtesy,
　　And look'd on me much sweeter,
Yet easy could I never be,
　　For thinking on Sir Peter.

---

* The Duke of Hamilton.

I fain would wear an easy air,
  But, oh ! it look'd affected ;
And e'en the fine Ambassador,*
  Could see he was neglected.

Tho' Poury left for me the spleen,
  My temper grew no sweeter ;
I think I'm mad, — what do I mean ?
  To follow cold Sir Peter !†

XLII.

BALMANNO.

WHAT charms can English Margaret boast
  To fix thy inconstant mind,
And keep the heart that I have lost ?
  O, cruel and unkind !

---

* The Earl of Stair.

† This and the following songs were composed by Annie, daughter of Sir James Mackenzie, Bart., a Senator of the College of Justice, bearing the title of Lord Royston. She is said to have inherited the wit of her grandfathers, the first Earl of Cromarty, and Sir George Mackenzie, of Rosehaugh, which in some cases overbalanced her discretion. Her lampoons excited as much hatred as mirth, and she met with those spiteful returns which such poetesses must ever expect. This lively lady had no children by her husband, Sir William Dick, of Prestonfield, Bart., and died in the year 1741. Her Phaon, whom she seems to laugh at in these verses, was Sir Patrick Murray, of Balmanno.—C. K. S.

For I can kilt my coats as high,
  And curl my red toupee——'
And I'll put on the English mutch,
  If that has charms for thee.

Let no nymph toss thy leathern fan,
  Nor damsel touch thy box ;
For I'll, Balmanno, have thee all,
  Even take thee with a . . . !

Since that's, alas ! thy woful case,
  There's none so fit as I ;
For ne'er a lass in all the land,
  Can boast more mercury.*

XLIII.

MRS. MITCHELL AND BORLAN.

" Who's that at my chamber door ? "
  " It's I, my dear," quo' Borlan ;
" Come in," quo' she, " let's chat awhile,
  You strapping, sturdy Norlan."

---

* Written after a raffle, in which Sir Patrick gained a fan and a snuff-box. English Margaret was Lady Margaret Montgomerie, daughter to the Earl of Eglintoune, and afterwards the wife of Sir James Macdonald, of Slate. She is termed English, because she was educated at a boarding-school near London.—C. K. S.

Fair Mitchell needed add no more,
   For Borlan straight did enter,
And on his knees he vow'd and swore,
   For her he all would venture.

Fair Mitchell answer'd with a blush,
   " Your love I don't intrust, sir,
But should it reach my father's ear,
   How would he puff and bluster ! "

" O, let him bluster as he will,"
   Replied the amorous lover;
" If you'll consent my arms to fill,
   Let him go to Hanover."*

---

* From circumstances, I suspect this song to be the
composition of Lady Dick, but am not certain..

THE END.

www.ingramcontent.com/pod-product-compliance
Lightning Source LLC
Chambersburg PA
CBHW020030030726
47499CB00007B/2354